Sally Prue

James and the Alien Experiment

Illustrated by Steve May

A & C Black • London

Reprinted 2006, 2008
First published 2005 by
A & C Black Publishers Ltd
38 Soho Square, London, W1D 3HB

www.acblack.com

Text copyright © 2005 Sally Prue
Illustrations copyright © 2005 Steve May

The rights of Sally Prue and Steve May to be identified as the
author and illustrator of this work have been asserted by them in
accordance with the Copyrights, Designs and Patents Act 1988.

ISBN 978-0-7136-7457-6

A CIP catalogue for this book is available from the British Library.

This book is produced using paper that is made from wood grown in
managed, sustainable forests. It is natural, renewable and recyclable. The
logging and manufacturing processes conform to the environmental
regulations of the country of origin.

Printed and bound in Great Britain by Bookmarque Ltd, Croydon.

Chapter One

One afternoon, James Hunter was kidnapped by aliens.

He was just sitting quietly in his living room when the television started making *shpitch*! *shpitch*! noises, and then some writing appeared on the screen:

YOU ARE ABOUT TO BE KIDNAPPED BY ALIENS

it said.

PLEASE DO NOT ADJUST YOUR SET

The screen had gone a shining, swirly green, like washing-up liquid. And then the swirls came together, until it looked as if a bony hand was reaching out of the set.

Another trailer, thought James.

Boring.

It did look real, though. It was a really good special effect: but if the programme was any good, if it was really *scary*, then it would be on after bedtime and he wouldn't be allowed to watch it.

Some more writing came up on the screen:

WE APOLOGISE FOR ANY INCONVENIENCE

it said.

And then, the bony hand zoomed right out of the screen *and grabbed him*.

James couldn't believe it: a massive green thumb and forefinger had clamped themselves round his waist. And as he stared down, frozen in horror, it lifted him out of his chair.

'Oi!' he said. 'What do you think you're doing? Let me go! Let me – *oof*!'

James put up his arm to protect his head from the glass of the television screen, but it seemed to have vanished. He caught a glimpse of a thicket of multicoloured wires as he was pulled right into the television. He struggled like mad, but the bony hand was as hard as rock and he couldn't get away.

James was going ever so fast, though he had no idea where he was going. He was going so fast that at first everything was blurry, but after a few seconds he saw squares of blue and grey, and then, horribly far below him, a green rectangle. That was the football stadium, right on the other side of town.

Then something wet hit him right in the face. He spluttered, and wiped his eyes, and saw that there was a cloud underneath him, shining like a gilded cauliflower.

I'm being kidnapped by aliens, he thought; but he was too amazed to take it in properly.

There was something in the sky in front of him, now. It was a building – perhaps a spaceship – and it was glowing like the flames of a gas cooker.

I'm being kidnapped by aliens, he thought, again. And this time he believed it. He closed his eyes, and opened his mouth, and he screamed.

James was lying on something cold, and all around him were the tinking and purring sounds of machinery.

'Yuk,' said a voice, horribly close. 'It's *revolting.*'

James kept his eyes tight shut and hoped very hard that he was dreaming.

'Looks dead to me,' said another, deeper voice.

I'm asleep, thought James, gritting his teeth with the effort of believing it. *I'm asleep. I'm – OW!*

He opened his eyes hastily because something was poking him. There was a *thing* right in front of him. It was all green and slimy, and it had purple eyes and a small wobbly trunk.

James screamed again.

'Ah,' said the thing, blinking at him and seeming rather pleased. 'Good. Not dead, after all. Right, then, let's get down to business.'

There were two of them. The one over at the control panel, who had six-inch eyelashes and sequins stuck on its antennae, pressed a gleaming silver button and something began to go *tinkerty-tonk*.

'Let me go!' said James, wildly. 'I want to go home!'

The nearest alien made tut-tutting noises. 'Nonsense,' it said. 'Why, this is your lucky day.'

James scrambled to his feet. Everything was shiny and round, like the inside of a huge washing machine. 'No, it's not!' he said. 'What … what do you want with me?'

'All sorts of things,' said the alien, grandly. 'I am Improver Trowpockle of the planet Terkle, and this is Assistant Improver Trada. We're going to redesign you.'

Chapter Two

'I don't know why you're screaming,' said Trowpockle, irritably. 'Honestly, we give up our time to fly round the universe spreading news of our scientific genius and helping all you aliens, and then you're ungrateful. Don't you understand we're here to do you a favour?'

'Yeah,' said Trada, who was dreamily painting her ear lobes a shiny bright blue. 'I mean, you're so ugly. No antennae. No slime. I mean, yuk!'

'Quite,' said Trowpockle. 'Now, what would you like us to do? We could change your legs into wheels. Or we could give you arms you can dig with. Think how nice that would be – why, if you wanted an extra room in your house you could dig yourself one in no time at all.'

'*I want to go home!*' said James.

Trowpockle waddled over to a stool and hoisted himself onto it. 'A tail?' he suggested. 'I find mine *very* useful – keeps me cool, and it's ideal for swotting bats. Or how about sharper teeth? Think of the pleasure of being able to help yourself to a passing badger whenever you felt hungry.'

James shuddered. 'I really do have to go home,' he said. 'My mum will be ever so worried.'

But Trowpockle shook his head.

'Oh, there's no need to worry about your mother,' he said. 'This ship is going nearly as fast as time, so that means you've only been gone a couple of seconds. Now, how about flying? That's always popular. Think of playing fighter pilots. Think of being able to drop stink bombs down nasty people's chimneys and then watch them come staggering out all green in the face and blaming each other.'

James hesitated. That did sound fun. 'If I could fly I'd be just like Superman,' he said, thoughtfully.

'That's right.' Trowpockle rubbed his paws together with satisfaction. 'We'll add one improvement each day, so we can monitor exactly what effect it's had, but you can have any superpower you like. Super-smell, perhaps? Just think, once you've got that you'd never tread in dogs' mess again.'

James Hunter, Superboy? That was such an incredible idea that James's brain nearly seized up. What superpower should he choose? Definitely not super-smell, or his teacher's hairspray would seem even pongier, and he nearly suffocated whenever he went into Mrs Sharply's classroom as it was.

Something on one of the control panels began to go *beep-beep*. Trada put down her bottle of ear-lobe paint and squinted vaguely at the display. 'An oojit's flashing,' she reported. 'The sort of dial thing with pointers on.'

'Ah. The clock, you mean.'

'Oh yeah. Yeah, that's right, I remember now. It's for telling the time. And that buzzer thing means that if we don't hurry up we won't be able to send him back today.'

Being able to fly would be completely brilliant. If James could fly he'd be able to get into the football every week for free… But then x-ray vision would be really neat as well. With x-ray vision he'd be able to sort out the best soccer-card packs before he paid for them.

'Countdown,' announced Trada. 'Nine minutes fifty five. Nine minutes fifty. Nine minutes forty five…'

James was trying his hardest to decide, but his brain was so cluttered up with incredible ideas that it just kept going *wow-wow-wow-wow-wow*! like Dad's car on a cold morning.

'You'll have to hurry,' said Trowpockle. 'We could make you a more attractive colour, if you like. A nice smart green, perhaps.'

James shook his head. The trouble with deciding was that he was a slow sort of person when it came to thinking. He liked to consider things carefully. He'd often wished he were quicker, but—

Yeah! *That* was what he'd have. That would be *brilliant*. James felt a huge grin spreading over his face at the thought of it.

'Super-speed,' he said. 'That's what I want. I want to be the fastest person in the entire world.'

Trada pressed loads of buttons, and James was so excited he could hardly breathe.

'You'll fall asleep for a while,' Trowpockle told him, 'and when you wake up you'll be back home in your armchair. You might even think this has all been a dream, until your incredible super-speed starts working tomorrow morning.'

'How fast am I going to be?' asked James, his heart pounding like mad.

'Oh, fantastically fast. Faster than anyone's ever been. Ready?'

James swallowed down a big lump of excitement. 'But what if something goes wrong?'

'Oh, don't worry, we'll bring you back up here tomorrow night for a checkup, and then if anything's not working we can fix it, or even reverse the process. Everything ready, Miss Trada?'

'Well, I've plugged in the thingy.'

'Excellent. Here goes!'

And at that moment James suddenly realised properly what was going to happen: *aliens were about to start messing around with his body.* He opened his mouth to tell them to stop, but Trowpockle was pulling down a big handle on the control panel and it was too late. Huge geranium-coloured explosions zapped his brain into little pieces – and then everything went black.

Chapter Three

What a dream! thought James, blinking uncertainly at the television. The News was on, so he must have slept straight through his cartoon.

'You've woken up, then,' said Mum. 'Sound asleep, you were. I thought I was going to have to carry you up to bed.'

James sat himself up. 'My arms and legs feel as if they've got maggots wriggling about inside them,' he said.

'That's just pins and needles,' said Mum. 'It'll be the way you've been lying.'

But it didn't feel like pins and needles. Bits of him kept twitching when he wasn't expecting it, and his skin felt shuddery, and a little sore.

I must still be half-asleep, he thought.

He made some excuse to Mum and went to bed.

James woke up next morning from the deepest sleep ever to hear Mum thumping on his bedroom door.

'James! James! Are you awake?'

James managed to haul up a groan.

'Well, rise and shine, then!' called Mum. 'It's twenty past!'

James didn't want to get up. He'd had horrible dreams about maggots all night and he just wanted to lie there and be glad they were gone.

'James!' called Mum, again.

'Coming,' he said, lying comfortably in bed.

The door handle suddenly turned and his bossy big sister Tina poked her head round the door. She was looking mad and vicious, but that was mostly because of her purple hair, inch-long false nails, and the tattoo on her neck.

'Mum!' she called, down the stairs. 'He's still in bed!'

There were rumbling sounds of Mum coming up the stairs and James lost all desire to lie in. Mum had been known to come up and squeeze a cold flannel over him. He leapt out of bed, pulled off his pyjamas, jumped into his clothes, brushed his hair, pulled the curtains, straightened his duvet, hid various bits of junk under his bed, and put his dirty clothes in his laundry bag.

Mum was making flannel-wetting noises in the bathroom. James stood in his tidy room and breathed. It was fantastic. It was tremendous. All that about the aliens was true, and it had *really worked*. He, James Hunter, was *the fastest person on Earth*.

When Mum came in, with a dripping cold flannel and a grim face, she found James all dressed and ready.

'Oh!' she said, put out. 'Tina said you were still in bed.'

'I was just … er … having a lie-down,' said James.

'But you've only just got up!'

'It was very tiring tidying my room,' said James. And Mum laughed and told him to hurry up and come down to breakfast, or his egg would be stuck to the plate.

Mum paused in the doorway. 'There's a funny smell in here,' she said.

James couldn't smell anything.

'It's as if something's scorching,' she said. 'You haven't been playing with matches, have you? We don't want you setting the house on fire.'

'No,' said James, who hadn't. The matches were kept in the medicine cabinet and he hadn't worked out how to pick the lock, yet.

Mum shrugged. 'Funny,' she said. 'I'll have to check your electric blanket.'

James ate up all his eggs and bacon, and then he had seven slices of toast.

'You're disgusting,' said Tina, biting into her fourth piece of crispbread.

'You haven't got time for any more, James love,' said Mum. 'You'll be late for school.'

James helped himself to a couple more slices of bread and a chocolate biscuit while Mum's back was turned. It was funny, but he could never remember feeling so hungry in his life.

He left for school at three minutes to nine.

Mum was freaking out by then. 'You'll be late,' she said, for the twelfth time, 'and then we'll be in trouble with Mrs Sharply. Be off with you.'

James's previous record for running to school was five and a half minutes, but that day he did it in *under 30 seconds*. Mum had been right, though, there *was* a scorching smell about, and it was so strong by the time he got to school that James was beginning to be quite hopeful that the buildings might have burned down in the night. But when he turned the corner the school wasn't even singed at the edges.

In assembly, while Mr Halford the headteacher read them the coffee-pot story for the millionth time, James tried to make plans to show everyone his super-speed.

The trouble was, he was so hungry all he could think about was food. It was weird still being hungry after that enormous breakfast. It was almost as if all the maggots in his arms and legs had wriggled into his stomach and were devouring everything he ate. James was reduced to chewing his nails, but they were already bitten nearly down to the pink bits, and anyway, they were never very filling.

He was so desperate by the time assembly had finished that he got Theresa Wodgett to sell him part of her sweet hoard. It cost him fifteen pence just for one measly Slurp Bar, but at least it kept him alive until ten o'clock, by which time he was so hungry he was feeling dizzy.

'Are you all right?' asked Simon Boggis, who sat next to him in class. Simon was plump, dark, slow, and James's best friend.

James shrugged. 'I got kidnapped by aliens last night and they've given me super-speed,' he explained.

'Oh,' said Simon. 'That's nice.'

'I suppose so,' said James. 'But it's making me ever so hungry.'

'Silence!' snapped Mrs Sharply.

Mrs Sharply was thin and spiky, and she was the nastiest teacher in the school. She was probably the nastiest teacher in the *whole world*. She hated everybody, especially children. She used to spend all day reading books about ladies in silly long dresses, and while she read them she used to make the class work in silence for hours and hours.

James put his head in his hands. He was suddenly so weak with hunger that he couldn't hold his head up any longer.

'Please, Miss,' said Simon. 'I don't think James is feeling very well.'

Mrs Sharply gave James a revolted look through her winged spectacles. The class reckoned she had wings on her spectacles because there was nowhere at school for her to park her broomstick.

'Well, go to the secretary, boy,' she said, waving him away. 'Don't breathe your revolting germs around here!'

The school secretary had the kindest smile anyone had ever seen; so James told her all about the aliens, and she asked him if he thought he needed something to eat.

'Oh yes,' said James, who was feeling so empty he was beginning to worry that his trousers might fall down. So she gave him four biscuits from the staff-room tin, and he promised not to tell anybody in case she got into trouble. Then he went back to class.

James managed to get through the next hour by nibbling the end of his pencil and biting his nails until his fingers were sore.

At playtime, instead of playing football, he had to go round borrowing food. He stuffed himself solid with two Crunchoes, three Yummies, four CaloriBars, five Licksy Biscuits, and a large packet of Jelly Eels.

Simon watched him curiously. 'It's going to be expensive, you having super-speed,' he said. He was helping by unwrapping the sweets so James could get them down faster. 'And you'll get thousands of holes in your teeth.'

James crammed the last chocolate bar into his mouth and nodded. He felt horribly sick, and his knees were looking ever so knobbly, but he thought he should last until lunch time without actually turning into a skeleton.

'I'm glad they didn't choose me,' said Simon, thoughtfully.

Chapter Four

James didn't get a chance to use his super-speed until lunch time because of Mrs Sharply. Mrs Sharply was *dangerous*. Her eyes were so cold with loathing that she could freeze your innards right from the other side of the classroom. She could make people cry just by raising her eyebrows, and if anyone made a noise she made everybody write lines all through playtime.

Simon Boggis's big brother said that once Mrs Sharply kept a boy behind after school, and when he came out his hair was white and he'd gone mad with terror.

As soon as the dinner bell went, James rushed to the canteen at super-speed to eat five helpings of everything. The canteen had that funny scorching smell, too, but all the food was lovely.

James went out to play once the serving

hatches were closed. He felt ever so full of custard, but he didn't care because this was the moment he'd been waiting for. This was when James could show everybody that he was now the best footballer in the world.

He was, too. It was wonderful. He could run rings round people – whizz round them till they were dizzy. He could zoom by and take the ball, even from big boys like Chunky Baxter, and once he'd *got* the ball no one could catch him.

It was fantastic – splendid – magnificent. Like being every member of United all rolled into one. He scored *ten* goals. It was so beautiful that if he'd been a girl he would have cried.

'Here,' said Chunky Baxter, suspiciously. 'How come you're so good all of a sudden?'

Chunky Baxter was all right, really – it was just that his hobby was thumping people. He didn't do it to hurt them – it was just something he did. And Chunky Baxter was big. *Really* big.

James looked up at him and wondered if scoring ten goals against Chunky had been the best idea he'd ever had.

'It's because he was kidnapped by aliens who gave him super-speed,' explained Simon, helpfully.

'Oh,' said Chunky. 'That explains it, then.' He began to walk off, but then he stopped. 'I've never thumped anyone who's been kidnapped by aliens,' he said, thoughtfully.

James felt as if someone had put all his helpings of custard in a cement mixer. *Kerflump* it went.

He began to back away.

'Come here,' said Chunky Baxter, mildly. People didn't bother to run away from Chunky Baxter because his great heavy legs could go at a tremendous speed.

James was just about to give himself up, when he thought: *super-speed*.

He went off like a rocket. It was incredible: the whole school just stood there with mouths wide open. He could run so fast that by the time Chunky Baxter worked out where he was, James had been round the playground twice.

He went faster – as fast as he could go. Everything went blurry. He could go so fast it was almost like flying, and the only slightly worrying thing was that the scorching smell had come back.

And at that moment his socks burst into flames.

James yelped and jumped in the air.

All the girls screamed, but Simon shouted, 'The pond, James! The pond!' and James zipped across the playground at super-super-speed and jumped right in.

The pond was ice-cold. James stood there cooling off his scorched ankles, with the mud gradually enveloping his shoes, and terrible images filled his mind. What if there hadn't been a pond?

'What's going on?' asked Mrs Sharply, scowling, looking up from where she was sitting on a bench reading her book.

Mrs Sharply was horrible. When Simon tried to explain about the aliens, he was sent to stand in the corridor, and James had to change into the most horrible clothes in the accident cupboard and spend the rest of lunch time sitting at his desk with his arms folded.

James didn't mind. He was afraid to move in case he burst into flames again.

'Are you all right?' Simon asked, when the bell had gone. He'd brought James a bagful of leftover baked potatoes that he'd begged off the dinner ladies.

James had been scared stiff, soaked through, and now he was starving again. 'I'm going to have to get the aliens to take off my super-speed,' he said, glumly.

'Perhaps they'll give you something better, instead,' said Simon. 'Perhaps they'll turn you into a monster and then you can eat Mrs Sharply.'

'I'd rather eat mouldy cowpats.'

'Well, you could just *frighten* her, then,' Simon suggested, hopefully. 'Just so her hair stands on end and her eyes fall out and she runs screaming out of school and she's never seen again.'

James suddenly felt much happier.

Mrs Sharply.

His super-speed had got him into a lot of trouble, but perhaps, if he thought and thought, he'd be able to work out something interesting to do about Mrs Sharply.

She appeared in the classroom door at that moment, fixed them with lizard eyes, and sent them to stand in corners, for talking.

That gave James a chance to make plans.

He was going to have one last run at super-speed before he finished with it for ever.

Chapter Five

Mrs Sharply drove a posh white car. Mr Sharply, who was ever so bald and thin and frightened-looking, had won the lottery the year before, and Mrs Sharply had gone out and bought herself a big car and a fur coat. She made poor Mr Sharply stay at home and do the housework, except for sometimes when she needed him to carry things. Everybody felt very sorry for him.

James waited by the school gates for a long time before he was rewarded by the sight of Mrs Sharply. Her car set off its alarm in panic when it saw her, but she subdued it with a couple of kicks from her spiky shoes.

James waved to her as she hurled the poor car, tyres screaming, round the corner. She only scowled at James, of course, but that didn't spoil his plan. He nipped along at super-speed until he got to the end of the road and then he stood by the kerb and waved again.

She looked at him twice, that time.

The *third* time he waved to her, on the pelican crossing outside the chemist's, she was beginning to look a bit cross-eyed. Good. James put on another super-speed spurt.

They were resurfacing the road just along from there. There were steaming cauldrons of tar, and heaps of stuff like half-melted liquorice that were raked tenderly across the road and then squashed by steamrollers into sleek blackness. James thought it was wonderful.

The workmen were busy drinking their tea, so they didn't notice James when he nipped out in front of a bubbling cauldron and waved at the posh white car that was coming down the road.

This time Mrs Sharply's face went white, just as if she'd seen a ghost. Yes, that was it – *the ghost of James Hunter.* James pulled his face into a ghastly grin and held his droopy hands above his head like ghosts did.

Mrs Sharply's eyeballs nearly fell out. She screamed so loud that James could see right down her throat to the little dangly bit, and then she pointed the car at him and put her foot down on the accelerator.

If James hadn't been super-fast she might have got him, but he just managed to zip out of the way and over a hedge.

Mrs Sharply's car hit the cauldron with the biggest *crunch* James had ever heard. The cauldron rocked, balanced precipitously, swung round, and crashed over, splattering black tar everywhere. The car reared up on its back wheels, just missed the steamroller and ended up across the road with its bonnet half open, as spotty as a Dalmatian.

It took Mrs Sharply a little while to find her way out of the car, because the door locks had all jammed. She had to climb out through the boot in the end, and she got tar all down her skirt.

James hung around to hear what the workmen had to say. They were terribly rude – worse than Dad when he was putting up shelves, even – but when Mrs Sharply tried to move in close to zap their insides with a close-range blast of her horror-vision, it turned out that her heels had sunk right into the new road surface and got stuck. She had to go home in her bare feet. It was ever so funny.

But then Mrs Sharply happened to catch sight of James through the hedge. And she looked so mean that his bones turned to jelly.

He took off, and he didn't stop running till he'd got home and had slammed the door behind him.

Tina sniffed at him as he stood panting in the hall. 'Mum!' she called. 'James has been smoking! He *stinks*!'

Mum hurried in. 'You haven't, love, have you?' she asked, sniffing as well. 'You don't want to start that – cost you a fortune, that would. *And* it'll give you wrinkles.'

'No,' said James. 'I haven't been smoking. Mum, what's for tea? I'm *starving*!'

Tina pointed a long, accusing fingernail at him. 'All his clothes are singed,' she said. 'Just look at his trousers.'

James looked down hastily at his clothes the school secretary had dried for him. The hems of his trousers were brown, and so was the front of his jersey. Whoops.

Mum looked at him searchingly. 'How did it happen, love?' she asked.

James tried to think of something to say, but he was so hungry all he could think of was food. Lovely lovely lovely food: golden fishfingers and tasty beans.

'I was watching the road men melting the tar over their fire,' he said.

'*Moron*,' said Tina, tossing back her purple hair. 'You're always hanging about getting in the way, you are.'

'Mrs Sharply drove into a big cauldron of tar,' said James, suddenly tremendously happy, despite feeling as if his skin was shrinking over his bones. 'It went all over her car, and when she got out, her shoes got stuck in it.'

And then all of a sudden Tina was grinning, too.

Mum shook her head. 'We'll just have to hope the singe marks wash out,' she said. 'But you keep away from fire in future, love. It's dangerous.'

Super-speed had been quite fun, some of the time; but James was ever so glad he was getting it taken off.

'Don't worry, Mum,' he said, as he made his way to the kitchen. He'd have an enormous tea, and then he'd settle down in front of the TV to wait for the giant hand. 'It won't happen again.'

'But what was wrong with it?' asked Trowpockle, rather offended, as James scrambled up from the shiny floor of the spaceship.

'It made me hungry,' said James, 'and my clothes caught fire.'

Trowpockle's trunk lifted alertly. 'We could give you fireproof fur,' he offered. 'Guaranteed up to 1,000 miles per hour.'

'No, thank you,' said James.

Trowpockle tut-tutted and shook his head. 'Oh, all right, we'll take it off then,' he said. 'So what shall we try next? Horns? Would poison glands come in useful, do you think?'

James shuddered. 'No, thanks.'

Trowpockle heaved a sigh. 'Goodness knows what the rest of you humans are like,' he said wearily, 'if you're the best there is.'

'Am I really the best?' asked James, very pleased. 'The best in the whole world? Why?'

'Because you're young, for one thing – grown-ups are hopeless. Once they find they're in a spaceship they just go rigid and make howling noises – and you're absolutely average in every way.

'Now, how would you like a small trunk?' He squinted down modestly at his own. 'Perhaps one rather like mine. It's useful for getting that last bit of milkshake out of the glass, and it makes a small but efficient vacuum cleaner.'

'Not on your nelly,' said James.

A beeping noise sounded through all the ticking and whirrings of the ship.

'We're nearly out of range,' said Trada, through her chewing gum.

'Well, we'd better get on then,' said Trowpockle. 'So what will you have, young human?'

'I don't know,' said James. 'I've been thinking about it for ages, but I can't decide. I mean, I thought super-speed would be a good idea, and look at all the disasters *that* caused. You should have chosen someone cleverer, who could work out what would be the best thing to choose.'

'Nine minutes zero. Eight minutes fifty five.'

Trowpockle suddenly smiled. 'Let's give you some *super-brains*, then,' he said.

Trada groped for the Instruction Book. 'Coming up,' she said.

James gaped. 'Super-brains?'

'That's right,' said Trowpockle. 'Just what you need. Now, super-brains are a bit different from super-speed. For one thing, they'll take effect almost as soon as you get home.'

'So … I'm going to be really clever?'

'Oh yes, fantastically clever. Your brains are going to be stuffed absolutely full of incredible intelligence. Are we ready, Miss Trada?'

'Yeah. Well, I *think* I've pressed the right button.'

'Off we go, then.'

James suddenly realised what was going to happen: *aliens were about to start messing around with his brain*. He opened his mouth to tell them to stop – but geranium-coloured patterns were erupting inside him, and it was too late.

Chapter Six

James woke up in his armchair feeling as if his head was full of electrically charged brillo pads. He sat himself up cautiously.

'You're turning into a real dormouse,' said Mum, who was sitting knitting in front of the News. 'This is the second time I've found you asleep in front of the TV. You're not ill, are you?'

James blinked and tried to work out why he was feeling so peculiar.

Super-brains?

'I'm all right,' he said, wondering if it was true.

'Good.' Mum was counting stitches. 'Your jumper's coming on quite fast, look. I must be nearly half-way up the back.'

The electric brillo pads in James's head started sizzling away like sausages, and then his hand was picking up Mum's knitting pattern, and he was *understanding* it. It was weird. Before he knew what was happening the brillo pads were working out the most horribly complicated sums.

And here was the answer.

'You have 98 more rows to knit,' he heard himself say. 'That means that you have completed 33.75 per cent of the back of the jumper.'

Mum goggled at him.

'Or, to put it another way,' James went on, horrified at the stuff coming out of his mouth but somehow unable to stop himself, 'you are 74.21 per cent to where the sleeves should be set in.'

'Am I?' asked Mum, vaguely appalled.

James's brain was now working out something called a standard deviation, and he didn't know how to stop it. It was horrible: it was like having maggots in his brain, and they kept squiggling about.

He staggered off to bed.

In assembly the next day James's brain worked out how many feet of parquet flooring there were in the school hall, and then estimated the number of hairs left on Mr Halford's head.

'You all right?' asked Simon, as they filed out.

James shook his head. 'Those aliens have gone and given me super-brains,' he said. 'They've made me really really clever.'

'Oh,' said Simon. 'What's it like?'

'Horrible,' growled James. He'd got hardly any sleep the night before because his brain had kept on working out stupid things like the average time it took his family to use up a toilet roll. 'It's like having dancing maggots in your head.'

'Oh,' said Simon, again, mystified.

Mrs Sharply was in an particularly vicious mood that morning because her car was being mended and so she'd had to come in on the bus. She'd devised an especially cruel torture for the class. They had to add up all the numbers from one to *100*. The class sighed, but James's brillo-pad brain had worked it all out before he'd even written the date.

It was easy: the numbers from one to 100 could be made into 49 pairs – one and 99, two and 98, and so on – and they all added up to 100. Left over would be the numbers 50 and 100. So that made … 5,050.

He wrote it down and then leant back to try to catch up on a bit of sleep. But his brain didn't *want* to sleep. It kept chuntering on about the number of tufts in the carpet.

'James *Hunter*!' snapped a voice.

James hastily opened his eyes.

'Why aren't you doing your work?' demanded Mrs Sharply, fixing him with her evil-ray spectacles.

'Because I've finished it, Miss.'

The class gasped in wonder.

'Some aliens have given him super-brains, Miss,' said Simon, helpfully.

Mrs Sharply told Simon he was stupid and set James to scrubbing out the paint cupboard. And being clever didn't help with that at all.

'I can't stand it!' exclaimed James, wildly, at lunch time. 'My brain keeps going on and on at me about really boring stuff: it's like living with a dozen nagging grannies!'

Simon went pale at the thought.

Mrs Platt, the nicest dinner lady, noticed James's harrowed look and asked him if he'd like to lie down.

'He's not ill,' explained Simon. 'He was kidnapped by aliens and they've given him super-brains. He feels as if he's got maggots dancing in his head.'

'Oh dear,' said Mrs Platt, comfortably. 'These aliens get everywhere, nowadays. Why don't you go and play football? It'll take your mind off it.'

James tried, but it didn't work. His brain kept working out horribly complicated sums about angles of curvature and backspin, and the ticking in his head meant he couldn't concentrate on what he was doing.

'You're rubbish at football, today,' said Chunky Baxter.

'I know,' said James, sadly. 'It's my super-brains. I'm incredibly clever, and all the thinking doesn't leave any space for ball skills.'

'Oh,' said Chunky. 'Well I'm glad I'm stupid then.'

Some of James's class had gathered round to gawp at him.

'Hey, James!' said Ashfaq. 'What's 302.5 divided by 6.2?'

Fizz-fizz-fizz-ting!

'48.790322,' said James, miserably.

Ashfaq checked it on his watch calculator. 'Wow!' he said.

James put his hands over his ears. 'Don't ask me any more,' he said. 'It makes my head feel all squirmy and horrible.'

'*I'm* going to ask him a square root,' said Veronica, importantly. 'That's the most difficult sort of sum in the whole world. James, what's the square root of 7.1?'

James didn't want to answer, but his brain had worked it out and the answer was wriggling out over his tongue. '2.6645825,' he gulped.

'*Correct*,' said Ashfaq, in awe, poking at his watch. 'James knows *everything*!'

'I don't, I don't,' said James, desperate to scratch the itchy maggots in his brain and not knowing how. 'It's just that I can work stuff out, that's all.'

People began to look thoughtful.

'Could you work out how to get rid of Mrs Sharply?' asked Simon.

James clamped his mouth shut, but the pressure of the cleverness inside him was rising like an enormous burp. 'A bomb would do it,' he said, unable to stop the words.

'*Wow*,' said Ashfaq. 'A bomb would be *fantastic*. Do you know how to make one?'

And James did. It was terrible.

'I do!' he squeaked. 'Everything we need is in the caretaker's hut!'

Everyone was suddenly grinning – except

Veronica. 'Well, I think a bomb would be very silly,' she said. 'Someone might get hurt.'

'Yes,' said James. 'And we'd get put in prison for ages and ages, until we were as old as Mr Halford.'

Everyone stopped grinning.

'*Why* is there always some stupid snag?' asked Ashfaq.

'*Why* can't we have a nice teacher?' asked Simon, with a sigh.

And at that James's maggots were fizzing and squirming again. They did wild somersaults and acrobatics. It was horrible – like watching a close-up action movie on fast-forward.

James clenched his teeth, but his maggotty thoughts were bursting out of him. 'We can!' he squeaked. 'We can give her a pill to rinse all the nastiness out of her!'

People looked questioningly at each other.

'How would we make it?' asked Simon.

And then a huge list of ingredients started coming out of James's mouth.

'*Three oak leaves, some belly-button fluff, a bit of chalk, a wet bogie, 100 grams of potato peelings…*'

His mouth stopped talking at last, and there was silence. Then a squelching sound.

'Well, I've got the bogie,' said Chunky Baxter.

James's fingers made the get-rid-of-the-nastiness pill quite easily. It looked like a stock cube, only slimier. Ashfaq bought a Slurp Bar from Theresa, dug out some of the cream, and put the pill inside.

It was easy to get Mrs Sharply to eat it. As soon as they got back to the classroom, Ashfaq let her see it, and she swooped on it at once.

'Greedy, revolting child,' she said, snatching the chocolate bar, and putting the whole thing in her mouth.

Mrs Sharply went green, to start with.

'I hope she doesn't puke it up,' whispered Simon, very worried.

And then Mrs Sharply went blue … then white … and then, incredibly, she *smiled*.

'Oh, what lovely, lovely chocolate,' she said. 'And just *look* at all your sweet little faces! I feel so *privileged* to be here with you *special* children. Sweet Simon, and adorable Ashfaq, and charming…'

She stopped speaking … and swayed a little … and then … she keeled over.

Veronica knew what to do because her mum was a nurse. 'Mrs Sharply's heart's not beating,' she reported, her ear to Mrs Sharply's bony chest.

'Is that bad?' asked Chunky, hopefully.

'Well,' said Simon. 'It does mean she's dead.'

'Could be worse, then,' said Ashfaq.

But James's super-brains were giving a horrible tickly squirm just by his left earhole and they were working out what was going to happen. 'People will say it's all our fault,' he said. 'They'll say she was poisoned.'

'But nothing we gave her was poisonous,' pointed out Simon. 'It *shouldn't* have killed her.'

But James's maggots had worked that out, too. 'She was so completely horrible that now all the nastiness has gone there's nothing left. Her heart's just an empty shell.'

'I don't want to go to prison!' wailed Veronica. 'It's not fair!'

James's brains did a million calculations. He thought so hard that the maggots turned into blowflies and buzzed round his skull until his teeth came loose. There was only one way out of this.

'I'm going to have to make an antidote,' he said, and he quickly mixed up some leftover ingredients with a bit of spit and threw the pellet into Mrs Sharply's mouth.

Mrs Sharply sat up at once. 'What are you all doing out of your seats?' she snapped.

'I've just saved your life,' said James, bravely.

'Nonsense,' snapped Mrs Sharply. 'Utter nonsense. You can't possibly think I'm stupid enough to believe that for a moment, James Hunter.'

James tried to keep his mouth shut, but the strain of not answering was pushing at his eardrums. 'Yes, I can!' he heard himself say, though his insides were shrivelling with horror. 'You're really incredibly stupid. Your brain has shrunk through reading so many silly books!'

The class stood round with expressions of mingled terror and delight, and James wondered if the easiest thing might be to drown himself in the pond.

Mrs Sharply put her face down level to his. 'Never forget that you are in my power, James Hunter,' she hissed, as she zapped ice-rays of nastiness through his innards. And then she made James stand on a chair at the front of the classroom all afternoon and do his sums on the whiteboard.

It wasn't fair, thought James, crossly, as his super-brains rustled about inside his head like mad hamsters. His hand wrote out columns and columns of stuff he couldn't understand, and he was just *desperate* to go home.

'What's all this?' demanded Mrs Sharply, at home time.

'It's how to build a time machine,' said James's mouth.

'Stupid boy!' said Mrs Sharply. 'Rub it all out at once!'

'I hope your dancing maggots get better,' said Simon, seriously, as they were putting their coats on.

'They will,' said James. 'I'm having them taken off this evening.'

He could hardly wait.

Chapter Seven

James usually watched the cartoons after school, but that day his brain made him switch over to a programme about the Budget. James had one burger, 156 beans, and 25 chips for tea, together with 132.5 cubic centimetres of bread.

'Mum!' said Tina. 'Tell James to stop messing about with his food!'

'What are you doing, love?' asked Mum.

James flushed, and put down his ruler. 'Only finding out how much milk is in my glass,' he said, lamely.

Tina made a *tcha*! sort of noise, but James didn't answer because his super-brains were working out the number of stupid things Tina said in an average day – 643.

He sat down to watch television again straight after tea. Luckily, Mum and Tina were looking through a stick-on fingernails catalogue, and Dad was delivering a lorry load of lentils to Leicester, so he had the room to himself. His super-brains were still muttering and nagging away. They worked out the number of flowers on the wallpaper, and approximately how *long* his portion of chips had been – 200 centimetres. Then, just as James was just about to try tearing his head off, the TV went all fuzzy and spitty and a bony hand appeared on the screen.

He saw the gas-ring glow of Trowpockle's spaceship with incredible relief.

Trowpockle was looking extra slimy, and terribly smug. 'So how did the super-brains go?' he asked.

'Terrible,' growled James. 'It's like having electric brillo pads in my head – either that or dancing maggots. Take it off.'

Trowpockle tut-tutted irritably and Trada, who seemed to have had her knees pierced since yesterday, picked up a magazine and began to leaf through it.

'Something else, then?' said Trowpockle, with a sigh. 'Any ideas?'

'It's all terribly difficult,' said James. His super-brains had thought of lots of possibilities, and he quite liked the idea of being turned into Mr Halford so he could give Mrs Sharply the sack. That would be tremendous fun – but Mum would be bound to notice the difference at breakfast time.

'You really are very trying,' observed Trowpockle, crossly. 'We give you the most wonderful opportunities—'

'—That keep landing me in trouble.'

'—And all you do is whinge. What happened to your spirit of adventure?'

'All those maggots ate it,' said James.

'Look, I think the best thing would be if you put me back to normal and just let me go home.'

Trowpockle walked round in a small circle. 'One more attempt,' he said. 'Just one more, and if that doesn't work out we'll give up on this stupid planet and go somewhere we'll be appreciated, all right?'

James thought about it.

One last attempt.

Perhaps he could cope with one more try as long as he knew it really was going to be the last.

'OK,' he said, slowly. He thought about it carefully. 'Flying sounds quite fun, I suppose,' he went on.

'Certainly,' said Trowpockle, rubbing his claws together. 'Easy. We'll just hollow out your bones, and redesign your ribcage, and then—'

'Oh no,' said James, hastily. 'Oh no you don't. You're not messing about with my bones.'

But what should he have? Something really cool. Super-what? Super-vision? Super-hearing? Super-strength?

Super-strength? Then he'd be the strongest person in the school. The strongest person in the world, probably.

His class had liked his super-speed and super-brains. They would love it if he had super-strength. Perhaps if he was super-strong then Mrs Sharply wouldn't be so scary, and he'd be able to put her in her place.

'Super-strength?' he suggested.

Trada stopped twisting bits of silver foil into her chest hair and tugged down the Instruction Book.

This time he'd be really careful, James decided. He'd hardly use his super-strength at all, to start with. He'd just try it out once or twice to see what happened.

Trada licked a scarlet claw, turned a page, and typed in a whole load of stuff very fast.

And then James changed his mind. He didn't want to be super. Of course he didn't. Being super just gave you super-sized problems. Why hadn't his super-brains worked that out before?

He opened his mouth to tell her to stop…
But he was too late.

James woke up the next morning and opened his eyes. His super-brains must have really tired him out yesterday, because even though the dancing maggots had shut up he was feeling ever so heavy and tired. It took a real effort to haul himself out of bed. He had an awful feeling that today was going to be a bad, bad day.

And then, as if to prove it, when he was brushing his teeth his toothbrush went and broke.

It wasn't fair, things like that happening, especially on top of the aliens.

He showed Mum. 'It broke,' he said, dolefully.

Mum looked at the ceiling. 'All by itself?'

'Yes,' said James, sighing. It had been a really nice purple toothbrush.

'Well, that's the first time I've ever heard of such a thing happening, James. Are you sure you weren't doing something silly with it?'

'Of course I wasn't!'

Mum sighed, then. 'Well, I haven't got time to talk about it now, James. I'm late. Make sure you slam the door as you go out, won't you?'

James staggered heavily downstairs, picked up his school bag, and let himself out.

He slammed the front door ... and the *door handle* came off in his hand.

He stared at it, even more cross and surprised than before. Now the door handle had gone and fallen to bits. Why was everything disintegrating round him?

And then he realised.

Aliens, he thought. *Super-strength.*

Oh *no*!

James kicked out crossly at the broken door handle. It zoomed up at 100 miles an hour and went *crash*! right through the wood of the door.

Oh *noooooo*!

James thought about trying to put it all back together, but the door had a big ragged hole in it and there was nothing he could do.

Oh well. Perhaps Mum and Dad would think it had been done by vandals. James opened the garden gate very carefully, shut it and latched it as gently as if it had been made of glass, and walked gingerly up the road.

That morning they started off with English. James's pencil point broke almost straightaway. He went and sharpened it, but even though he was really careful it snapped again after only a couple of words.

James was so strong it was *scary*.

He trudged up to the front of the classroom again, sharpened his pencil again, got a death-ray stare from Mrs Sharply again, and went back to his place.

Snap!

'What's up?' asked Simon, in the smallest possible whisper.

James held up his broken pencil. 'I'm super-strong,' he whispered back.

Simon gave a silent whistle and handed over a pencil sharpener.

'Thanks,' breathed James, grabbed it, and crushed it into a thousand pieces between his fingers.

Everyone in the class heard the *crunch*. A tiny whisper ran round the room: *he's super-strong!* The class was suddenly alive with hope. James was super-strong. Perhaps today they could somehow get their own back on Mrs Sharply.

James carried on with his work, very very gently so as not to break the point of his pencil again, and as he did he wondered what to do.

Chapter Eight

Chunky Baxter couldn't see what the problem was. 'Pull her head off,' he said, simply.

But James shook his head. 'I'm not touching her,' he said.

Everybody thought hard.

'You could frighten her so much that she runs away and falls over a cliff,' suggested Ashfaq, hopefully.

'How?'

'Go berserk. Tear up her desk.'

'Brilliant,' said James, scathingly. 'And what would Mr Halford say?'

'He won't mind,' said someone. 'He hates Mrs Sharply as much as we do.'

'Go on,' said everybody, longingly. 'It's only a desk. Go on, James! Do it!'

'OK, OK,' said James, crossly. 'I'll think about it.'

Super-strength was horrible: James had to be really careful in case he touched someone and broke their bones, and people kept coming up to him and hissing *do something*! and he didn't know what to do.

Simon was the only one who understood. 'Later,' he kept telling everyone. 'He's going to do it later. Leave him alone.'

By lunch time people were getting restless.

'You're rubbish,' said someone, nastily, in the playground. 'You couldn't *peel a banana*.'

Simon handed James his empty drinks can. James pinched it down to the size of an acorn and flicked it at the caretaker's shed. There was an awful elephant-screaming noise and the shed's walls fell outwards and the roof folded up – and then they all found themselves staring at the caretaker, who was sitting on a paint tin with a doughnut halfway to his mouth.

Everyone stood absolutely still, open-mouthed, until the echoes had died away.

No one pestered James after that. He tried telling Mrs Platt the dinner lady about the aliens, but she just said *never mind, dear*.

They had rounders that afternoon. James

was the first to be picked. Everyone chosen on James's side pranced out smirking, and the others trudged and sulked.

James managed to miss the ball completely on his first three goes, but the fourth time he misjudged the timing and just clipped it.

The ball went up like a missile. It went across the playing field, over the hedge, and right over the row of houses that backed

onto the school. It went so fast it made a whistling noise. The class watched in awe as it hit a faraway chimney, bounced back, whizzed close over their heads, pinged off the climbing frame, and landed with a thud amongst the bushes by the school entrance.

'*Wow*!' said the class, and '*tcha*!' said Mrs Sharply.

'You horrible boy,' she said. 'How dare you be so careless with school property? You will sit out of games for the rest of term. Now, go with Veronica and find that ball at once. And don't be too long!'

James slunk off across the playing field and Veronica skipped about and chattered beside him. 'Ooh,' she said, 'you are strong, James. James! James!'

'What?'

'Don't you think we ought to hold hands if we're going near the drive, James?'

James began to run and Veronica pattered along in her whiter-than-white trainers, squeaking, *Keep away from the parked cars, James!*' and '*Don't go near the mud, James!*'

James had thought it was going to take all afternoon to find the ball — assuming it hadn't bounced up again and gone into orbit — but it wasn't long before Veronica bounded up to him, all hair ribbons and bossy smirk.

'Look, I've found it,' she said. 'And I was terribly, terribly careful not to tread on the flower bed, as well. Come along now, James. Back to our rounders!'

James followed her grimly. It was quite

hard to keep up with her because his muscles were made of iron or something, and they weighed him down.

'Come *along*, James!'

James turned the corner by the pond, but then he was suddenly too tired to go any further. He leant ever so wearily against a silver birch tree to get his breath back…

…and it *fell over*.

James felt the ground heaving under his feet, and then the whole tree tipped and fell through the school hedge. To make matters even worse, it got tangled up in the wires of a telegraph pole, uprooted that, too, and, with an awful *twanging* and *boinging* of cables, the whole lot smashed and bounced down onto the road.

Something squawked – but it was only Veronica.

'You *naughty boy!*' she said.

James peered through the large gap in the hedge. In the big hole in the ground where the telegraph pole had been there were layers of even thicker cables, and they were all fizzing and spitting as if lots of electricity was leaking out.

69

Across the road an alarm started blaring. All the lights had gone out in the shops. There were no lights in the school, either. Even the lamppost on the other side of the hill, the one that had been switched on since James was in the Infants, had gone out.

Oh *no*! thought James, yet again.

He turned round very carefully and went back to his class.

As the whole school had no electricity, everyone had to go and sit in the hall for the Longest Assembly Ever. It was torture. James's heavy bones poked into the floor, but he didn't dare fidget in case he kicked someone.

At the end of school, James went home quickly before people could start going on at him again to do something about Mrs Sharply. Everything he did caused trouble, and he just couldn't *wait* to have his super-strength taken away.

He'd forgotten all about the damage to the front door. The hole in it looked even bigger and more splintery than before.

No more improvements, he promised himself.

Whatever happened, he wasn't having any more improvements.

James was searching very carefully in his pocket for his key when he realised he could hear something. It was a sort of rustling and it was coming from inside the house. He listened. It was quiet and stealthy, but there was no doubt about it.

Burglars!

All of a sudden James's heart was beating very fast.

It's all right, he thought. *I'm strong. I can sort out a burglar.*

He opened the door very gently and quietly. There was the rustling again; and again.

There was definitely someone in the house.

Chapter Nine

James took a cautious step into the hall. If he could catch a burglar he might have his name in the papers. He might get a medal, even.

James took another step forward ... and then he gulped.

There was a pair of big black burglary boots sticking out of the cupboard under the stairs.

It was ever so lucky he was super-strong. He'd have to be careful not to hurt the burglar too much, of course – it wouldn't do to break any bits off him. What James would do was yank the burglar out of the cupboard by the legs, and then he'd sit on the burglar until he'd given back everything he'd stolen; and *then* James would call the police, and loads of police cars would come screeching up and it'd be brilliant.

James tiptoed forward very very quietly ... and then he grabbed the burglar's ankles and pulled hard. It worked beautifully. The burglar shot out backwards, and James sat himself down quite gently on top of him. And all the burglar said was '*oomph!*' and lay still with his nose squashed into the carpet.

James sat and breathed, triumphantly; and when the burglar began to squiggle he said, '*You keep still or I'll break your arms off!*' in a deep, growly voice.

The burglar forced its head sideways and spat out some bits of carpet fluff. 'You total *moron!*' it said.

James blinked and looked at the burglar more closely. It had purple hair. It had long red fingernails. It had a tattoo on its neck.

Oh *nooooooooooo!*

'Get off me!' shouted Tina, in a voice even fiercer and more growly than James's.

Getting off Tina wasn't safe. But then neither was sitting on her until Mum came home.

James got up and retreated to the door of the sitting room.

Tina heaved herself to her feet.

'I thought you were a burglar,' said James, weakly.

Tina pushed back her hair from where it had got caught up in her mascara.

'You total *moron*,' she said again.

'I'm sorry, Tina,' said James, who really really was. 'But your head was in the cupboard!'

Tina brushed fluff off her black jumper. 'I was mending a fuse!' she snapped. 'All the electricity's off.'

'That was an accident,' said James, like an idiot.

Tina black eyes widened. She pointed an accusing finger at James; and then she let out a howl of real anguish. 'You've *broken one of my nails*!'

James turned and ran. He dived into the sitting room and slammed the door just as Tina's bulk hit it. The handle came off in his hand, but it was the part that made the door open, so it was a good thing. There was a loud thud and the door rattled, but James was rushing to turn on the television.

Hurry up, Trowpockle, he thought. *Hurry up!* But nothing happened – nothing at all. The TV screen stayed dead and black.

But of *course* it wasn't working. James had just gone and short-circuited the electricity supply for the whole district.

A bulky figure appeared outside the open window. It had a tattoo on its neck, a purposeful air, and a stepladder. It was Tina. She would climb in through the window and torture James. She'd pull his hair, and poke him with her incredibly sharp, new stick-on nails (the ones he hadn't broken), and he wouldn't be able to do anything back to her in case she fell to bits.

'I couldn't help it,' he said. 'Honestly.'

Tina kept on coming.

'Help!' screamed James, though there was no one to hear him.

Tina's massive hand was pulling open the window.

How long did it take to mend a simple thing like a capsized telegraph pole?

'Trowpockle!' yelled James. 'Trowpockle, you got me into this mess! Trowpockle, *help*!'

'Who's Trowpockle?' asked Tina, carefully manoeuvering her second leg through the window and jumping down to the floor.

'He's an alien. He keeps kidnapping me,' said James. '*Trowpockle*!'

Tina snorted. 'I wish he'd kept you, you little idiot.'

'Don't hit me,' pleaded James. 'Look, I'll ask Trowpockle to improve you, too, if you like. I'll ask him … I'll ask him to get rid of that tattoo on your neck.'

Tina's hand went up to it. 'It's a brilliant tattoo,' she said, scowling.

'Yes,' said James, 'but think how nice it would be if it wasn't there. Trowpockle could do that, easy.'

Tina looked at him. 'You must be mad,' she said, but there was a quiver of doubt in her voice.

The television made a sudden crackling

noise and swirls began to wave across the screen.

'Trowpockle!' called James. 'Trowpockle, come and get me!'

'Where does he take you?'

'Up to his spaceship. *Trowpockle!*'

The screen had gone washing-up liquid green. James braced himself for the horrible stomach-sickening feeling of the bony hand grabbing him. Any moment now…

Tina suddenly launched herself at him and threw her arms round his neck.

'Woomph,' he said. 'Gerroff! What do you think—'

But James was already miles above the town. He could see it, all green and blotchy beneath him. And here were the clouds, bashing him wetly in the face. And Tina was with him. Her mouth was wide open, but they were going so fast that her screams were being left far behind them; and here was the darkness of space, and the gas-ring glow of Trowpockle's spaceship, and then…

…and then they were there.

Chapter Ten

Trowpockle peered at them over his glasses. 'Dear me,' he said. 'What's this?'

James pushed Tina away; and Tina, with a squawk of amazement, slid the whole length of the ship and bumped into something that looked like a dishwasher.

'It's a sister,' said James, gloomily. 'She went and grabbed hold of me just before you did.'

Tina's eyes were bulging. 'It's a space monster,' she said. 'Oh no oh no oh no oh no oh no! Help! Help!'

'Interesting,' said Trowpockle. 'Who do you think will hear your cries for help?'

'No one, really,' explained James. 'She's just sort of hoping.'

'Ah! Well, never mind. How are you finding your super-strength, young man?'

James scowled. 'Horrible. Really horrible. Everything I touch falls to bits. I've already smashed up half our house.'

Trowpockle sighed, and took off his glasses. 'You know, you really are the most difficult species,' he said.

'Sorry,' said James, 'but there it is. In fact I've decided I'm quite well designed as I am, thank you very much.'

Trada looked up from painting her nostrils. 'Funny,' she said. 'That's what the whales said.'

Trowpockle hoisted himself onto his stool. 'Oh well,' he said, wearily. 'That's another 3,000 years of my life down the drain. I thought that pointing out how badly designed humans are would be a help to them, but it seems there's nothing we can do. Set the course for home, Miss Trada.'

But Tina had pushed herself up on one elbow. She'd even stopped gibbering. 'You could give me stronger nails,' she suggested. 'My fake ones are costing me a fortune.'

'No, don't, Tina,' said James. 'You'd probably have to cut them with a hacksaw.'

'It'd be better than having horrible bitten nails like yours!'

'Yeah, but what if you caught one on

something? You'd probably tear your finger off.'

Tina winced, but Trowpockle's ears had pricked up. 'Are you saying that it's wrong for your species to eat your nails?' he said. 'Well then. How about if I made them taste revolting?'

James tried to thing of a reason why not. He couldn't.

'Could you take off my tattoo, as well?' asked Tina, hopefully.

'Your tattoo?' echoed Trada. 'But that's really really cool, that is.'

'Yeah,' Tina agreed. 'It's great for when I want to be Club Queen of the Night; but it looks a bit weird with a bikini, you know?'

A buzzer on the console began to beep.

'We must be sending you back,' said Trowpockle. 'Anything else we can do for the human race, while we're here?'

'No,' said James, firmly.

'Quite sure?'

'Well – you could mend all the things my super-strength broke,' said James.

'No problem,' said Trowpockle. 'I'll send the hand down now. Anything else?'

James thought. 'You couldn't … you couldn't do something about Mrs Sharply, could you?' he asked, wistfully.

Trowpockle hesitated. 'Well, I suppose we could take her home with us, if you liked,' he suggested.

James's jaw dropped. Take Mrs Sharply away? Right away, to another planet?

'What would you do with her?' asked Tina, in an awestruck voice.

'Oh, freeze her, and make a working model of her to put in our museum. And then once we'd done that we'd pop her back down on Earth none the wiser.'

James had an awful edge-of-a-cliff feeling; but he still couldn't say anything.

'How long would she be gone?' asked Tina.

'Ooh, not more than 10,000 years, at the outside. That'd be all right, wouldn't it? I mean, no one would miss her, would they?'

James thought. Who would miss Mrs Sharply? Not anyone in the school. Not poor Mr Sharply.

James slowly shook his head. 'Our class has television first thing tomorrow morning,' he said, slowly.

'Right, we'll pick her up then. Oh, I do feel better knowing we're going to do something useful. Right, well, it's been nice knowing you. Ready, are you, you two?'

James sat himself down on the floor. He was ready.

Someone was talking. James took a deep waking-up breath and struggled to open his eyes.

'Bundle of life and energy, you lot, aren't you? The Dynamic Duo!'

James sat up. Tina was on the settee looking dopey, and Dad was standing in his coat smiling at them.

'What happened to the spaceship?' asked Tina, blearily.

Dad chuckled. 'I've always thought you lived on another planet, Tina, but I never knew you actually had a spaceship,' he said. 'Did it have little green men on it who went *beep beep*?'

Tina blushed. 'I dreamt a hand came out of the TV and took James and me up to a spaceship,' she said. 'And there were two aliens on it called Trowpockle and ... er—'

'—Trada,' said James.

'Yeah,' said Tina, 'and they... *How did you know that?*'

'I was on the spaceship, wasn't I?' said James; and Dad laughed, and wandered out to the kitchen.

Tina was staring open-mouthed at James.

Then she heaved herself up and went over to the mirror. She craned her head round to try to see the back of her neck.

'It's gone,' said James. Then he had another thought. He scanned his hands carefully, searching for a finger with a little bit of bitable nail on it.

'*Yuk!*' The taste of it was just revolting: it was like *broccoli-flavoured earwax*. It was so bad that James had to run to the sink to rinse his mouth out.

Tina caught him as he was raiding the fridge for something to take the taste away.

'You tell anyone I was on that spaceship,' she said, waving a fat finger in his face, 'and I'll kill you, OK?'

'OK, OK,' said James.

'So just forget it and pretend to be normal.'

That wasn't going to be hard, because he *was* back to normal: he was practically an ordinary boy again. No more bursting into flames; no more maggots keeping him awake; no more being afraid to hit Tina in case she fell to bits.

He found that he was grinning from ear to ear. 'It's great, isn't it?' he said.

Chapter Eleven

When James got to school the next day everyone wanted to know what new super-power he had.

'I'm just ordinary, now,' he said. 'I'm back to how I was, except that my nails taste of broccoli-flavoured earwax. The aliens are going home today.'

Everyone was ever so disappointed, and James had to promise to let them taste his nail clippings once his nails had grown a bit.

'Pity about Mrs Sharply,' said several people. 'That extra-long assembly we had yesterday because of the power cut meant you never got a chance to do anything to her, didn't it?'

James shrugged and kept quiet.

The first thing Mrs Sharply did in class that morning was to switch on the television. Then she pierced everyone with a sub-zero frown and settled down with one of her silly books. Everyone sighed and fixed their eyes on the screen.

Two minutes into the programme, a message appeared:

MRS SHARPLY IS ABOUT TO BE KIDNAPPED BY ALIENS

it said.

Simon looked at James in dismay. 'Mrs Sharply's getting *superpowers*?' he exclaimed, horrified.

'Simon Boggis, stop talking!' snapped Mrs Sharply. 'Everyone put your hands on your heads!'

The television had gone the colour of washing-up liquid, and now a withered hand was forming in the depths of the screen.

'I don't know who's been playing with the video recorder,' Mrs Sharply went on, viciously, 'but you'll all be staying in until I find out!'

You could see all the bones in the hand, now.

'Miss!' shrieked Veronica, losing her head,

'Miss, Miss, it's aliens! They're coming to get you!'

'Veronica, don't be silly. Everyone knows there are no such things as – *ooooooooooomph!*'

The whole class sat, silent with wonder.

'Er – I'm looking for Mrs Sharply,' said a voice, mildly, behind them.

It was poor Mr Sharply, looking even thinner and more worried than usual. He was carrying an enormous pile of silly books.

'Some aliens have just kidnapped her,' explained Simon, into the silence.

Mr Sharply blinked. 'Oh,' he said. 'Er – why?'

James found that he was smiling and smiling. *Good* old Trowpockle. 'They're going to freeze her and make a model of her for their museum,' he said, happily. 'And she isn't going to be coming back for 10,000 years.'

Mr Sharply stared at him as if he could hardly believe it. '10,000 years?' he whispered.

James suddenly realised what a shock this must be.

Whoops.

'10,000 years?' Mr Sharply said again. '*10,000 years*?'

Everyone in the class had their mouths wide open.

Then Mr Sharply suddenly threw out his arms and fifty frilly ladies sailed flapping through the air.

'*10,000 years*!' shouted Mr Sharply, at the top of his voice. '10,000 YEARS! *Yippee!*'

Mr Halford came along after a little while to see what all the noise was about. As far as he could make out, it was something to do with Mrs Sharply having resigned.

And that was such good news that he went back to his study and shouted *yippee!* himself.

Nobody heard him. Outside in the playground Chunky Baxter was charging around hooting like a baboon, and everyone else was jumping up and down with joy. And they were carrying James Hunter on their shoulders.

And they were all cheering their heads off.

About the Author

When I was young I lived in a house that contained almost no storybooks at all; but in a long row on a high shelf was a set of huge blue encyclopaedias. They were quite old, and far too much of them was about mining or machinery, but every so often there was a chapter of folk tales. I read these stories again and again, and one of them was about the time when all the unborn animals chose their special gifts from God. The hawk chose to have wonderful eyesight, and the lion to have sharp teeth – but man chose to have no gifts at all. Many years later this became the idea that started off *James and the Alien Experiment*.

I'm married, now, and have two daughters, but I still live in the same town in

Hertfordshire, and I'm afraid I still only really read the story chapters of my encyclopaedias.

As well as writing stories, I have lots of fun of helping some very nice people to play the piano. I also play the recorder and the bagpipes, and I enjoy reading, and walking, and talking, and drawing, and eating, and daydreaming.

I've written quite a few books, from novels for teenagers to books for children just learning to read. If you enjoyed reading about James, then you might like to read *Goldkeeper*, which is about a boy called Sebastian who has lots of adventures with gangsters. My first novel to be published, *Cold Tom*, won the Smarties Silver and Branford Boase Awards.

Time
AND AGAIN

Rob Childs

*"By a click of the clock, You can go in reverse,
Time and Again, For better or worse."*

With the discovery of a strange-looking
watch, twins Becky and Chris gain the
power to travel back in time. It's the
opportunity to relive events and put things
right. But trying to change the past doesn't
always work out as the twins intend.
Especially when class troublemaker
Luke is around…

Black Cats
Books to pounce on

Bryony Bell's Star Turn

FRANZESKA G. EWART

"It's just as well Yours Truly has a breathtakingly brilliant, scintillatingly surefire gem of an idea up her sleeve."

There's never a dull moment in the Bell household. Fresh from success on Broadway, they now star in their very own reality TV show. Plus there's the mystery of Ken Undrum's long lost love to solve, the Nativity play to rehearse, and Bryony has special plans to make sure the coming Christmas will be full of surprises...

Black Cats
Books to pounce on

Spooks Away

SUE PURKISS

*"Those who enter Inverscreech should be wary.
Those walls contain some deep, dark secrets."*

Young ghosts Spooker, Goof and Holly are off
to a remote Scottish castle to make a video
about how to haunt. But the castle turns out
to be less lonely than expected. The arrival of
a bunch of Americans and a series of spooky
goings on give the ghosts rather more to deal
with than they'd bargained for…

Black Cats
Books to pounce on